The Ultimate Steal

The Ultimate Steal

Nicholas James Zornow

Published by Nicholas James Zornow, 2023.

This is a work of fiction. Similarities to real people, places, or events are entirely coincidental.

THE ULTIMATE STEAL

First edition. December 6, 2023.

ISBN: 979-8227372031

Written by Nicholas James Zornow.

Also by Nicholas James Zornow

Beneath The Secret Oak Tree
Midnight Fright Fest
Personal Poetry
They'll All Fall Down
The Ultimate Steal
Me, Not Being Me
A Conversation With Myself
Silently Violent
From My Shallow Beating Heart
Three Of Me
Untitled
The Untold Stories Of...
Mr. C
The Cloud Of Christmas Day
Life With Love
Heartbeats
A Trip To The Devil's Hole
Everything Will Be Alright In The Morning
Populate
Tales from Nick
Red Rose Promise

Watch for more at www.books2read.com/njz.

Table of Contents

Written by

Nicholas James Zornow

"Success shall crown my endeavors"

M.S.

Prologue

Impending psychological doom was fast approaching and everyone knew it. The family was gathered all together knowing that they would be traveling home without one of their own.

As a mother wept in a hospital chair in the far back corner of the room, an old man was comforting his teenage granddaughter. Her eyes fluttered open weakly and to everyone's surprise.

She signaled to her mother, so she approached with something in her hand. Without the strength to hold the heavy object herself, Maria had her mother hand the unknown package to her grandfather.

He was shocked. Even in all of this chaos and sadness, Maria did not forget her grandfather's birthday. As he softly tore the wrapping paper off, he realized that she had done it again. She had managed to gift a present that was absolutely perfect.

The old man could not help but tear up. Maria had given him a leather-bound copy of a horror novel entitled "The Forgotten Soul" on the burgundy cover. The book was read by the two together. This copy had glimmering, shiny, gold edges to the pages. The old man's favorite book.

He gave Maria a somewhat tight hug, trying not to hurt her, as she was already in pain. Her arms that wrapped around her grandpa became limp and her heart would beat no more. Cancer had taken away a beautifully loved girl at the age of fifteen.

Still hugging Maria's deceased body, he began to sob. A tear ran down and dripped from his cheek and it landed on the dead girl's naked head. The old man lightly wiped the tear with his hankey and gave her a kiss.

The room became silent as all of Maria's family members huddled around her unsurprised, yet obviously still emotional. The old man had already left the room with his hankey in one hand and the book in the other.

He loved horror novels. Hence the present. This one he would keep for a lifetime.

Walking down the bleak and dismal hospital hallway, he dropped to his knees as the alarm went off.

Then, the boy woke up, startled. "Just a dream." He reassured himself. The old man, Maria and all the rest of the family. Just a dream, (or better put a nightmare) of an eleven-year-old boy as he sat up alert in his bed.

David sat in his bed for the rest of the night, as morning approached quite quickly. He was to be getting ready for his first day of the fifth grade.

Just a dream. Or was it?

1

David Had splashed cold water on his pale face as per his mother's request. She always took very good care of him, but now even better that his father had left his life after a nasty divorce.

Julie (David's mother) had a great big batch of French toast on the table. And David ate the whole thing, needing all the energy he could get after a long night.

"Do we have any coffee?" David asked, followed by a cheerful laugh from Julie. "Yes sweetie, but none for you. Have some orange juice. It'll pick you right up." A smile on her face as she recommended the OJ.

After neglecting the glass of juice due to a full stomach, David walked sluggishly to the front door and proceeded to the end of the driveway waiting for his school bus to arrive. With nerves in his belly along with the French toast, David asked his mother if he could be dropped off at school. A new school for the fifth grader.

Without hesitation he was granted his wish from Julie and off they went to Barker (David's new school for the year).

After a quiet drive, he gave his mother a kiss on the cheek, as he knew that he would miss her all day. But he had a school day, and his mother had a workday ahead of them.

After the kiss, and a wandering walk trying to find his classroom, this was it. The first day at a new school, a new grade, a new teacher and new classmates. The only thing missing was new friends.

2

"Hey buddy, go long." The boy ran as fast as his little legs could and caught the pass from his father.

One solid, happy memory. David had many and they were all running through his head at superhuman-like speed. It actually made him a little worried, his brain racing so fast. Just like his little legs, faster than they seem.

Flashes of John were relentless. But why today? Actually, it was every day. Every day since the separation of John and Julie.

David hated John, but he loved his father. Both the same person and both out of David's life.

The beginning of the day had already started and David, lost in his own mind, actually forgot that he was in school. The only thing that brought him back to reality was a fire drill. One to start the year off so the students had a good idea of what the process was like.

David took a quick glance at the chalk board and realized that he had been reminiscing the whole day so far, as he did not recognize the questions. Too much mind wandering had already put David slightly behind.

But after the efficient fire drill, lunch was next and David would try to forget about his father, John, and hopefully make connections in a cafeteria filled with strangers.

3

The lunchroom had not one friendly seat for young David. The rest of the day did not go as smoothly either. New grade... Check. New school... Check. New friends... Not so much. In fact, not at all.

When David took his sad, large lunges on the steps of the school bus to head home, he was hoping to see a friendly face look at him. He was actually hoping for any face to make eye contact. But the school bus proved to be much of the same.

Later in the day, after he had let himself in the house and waited for his mom to get home from work, he gave his golden retriever, Tucker, a big hug and locked himself in his bedroom. Tucker was the only friendly face that David had seen for hours.

The dog was already fed, so David locked himself in his bedroom with a weak shut of his door. Emotionally depleted, he took a picture out of his nightstand. It was of John. With teary eyes, he gave it a quick rip in half.

The picture of his father was the last one he had. David just couldn't stand to remember the neglect that John had put toward him, even though he thought of him throughout the day. Another disappointing face to look at.

Eventually, while hugging his soft, cushy pillow, David fell asleep and had woken to the sound of his mother's jingling keys at the front door.

She knocked on his door and let herself in. "Hey sweetie. I got pizza for dinner." Then, she saw the torn photo and knew that her son had had a rough day. Fed up with John, both family members sat at the small, round table of the two-bedroom apartment and ate a few large slices with extra sauce for dipping.

David's mother was hiding something. The new action movie he had wanted to see for the past month or two. Julie thought it would brighten his dismal day, but she was wrong. David only focused on getting his mother to let him stay home from school tomorrow. No luck.

"Tomorrow will be better, I promise." Julie spoke as she tucked her son in his small but cozy bed. "That's so cliché, mom." David responded. She gave a slight grin, acknowledging the wit of her young son and went in the kitchen for a glass of wine.

Shortly after the cork popped, David fell asleep and when morning came, it was time to see the unfriendly faces of his peers and hopefully they would see him differently. And how very different he would look after one courageous act that his mother nor the law would appreciate.

4

Stomach gurgling after the lack of consuming his lunch on this windy Thursday afternoon at school, David couldn't bare to struggle with his hunger for much longer.

He looks from side to side with a hint of sadness and desperation. Nothing was out of the ordinary. But one more look to his left, David saw a candy bar on his teacher's desk, just barely sitting on the edge.

Mrs. Dougley had turned her back to write the day's cursive lesson on the chalk board, then something happened to David. He was feeling tempted. Tempted to do something wrong for the first time in his eleven years.

Quietly, but quickly David tip toed halfway through the classroom and snagged the candy bar and rushed to the bathroom located in the back of the room. Along the way, his sneakers squeaked, and right after he had closed the bathroom door, Mrs. Dougley noticed his absence.

"David? Are you okay?" she asked after knocking on the door. David had responded to his teacher, stating that he had a bad stomachache. But, in actuality, it was quite the opposite. He was speedily chomping on the delicious treat that he had taken from Mrs. Dougley, while sitting on top of the urine-stained toilet seat.

After finishing the candy bar and waiting a few minutes in the bathroom to act like he had been ill, David walked calmly back to his seat, with his now bloated tummy pressing against his desk.

"Are you feeling any better?" asked the teacher from across the room. And the response was... "Yes. A lot better." Words spoken with a grin on his face.

But, with the grin still on his face, two students, Chris and Eric gestured to David that they knew what he had done as they pointed to the chocolate on the left side of his bottom lip, as they sat in the same row of desks.

David had taken from his teacher and there were two young boys who knew it. The only thing that could be done now is damage control. How can David convince the two instigators to not tell on him? He had to figure that one out quickly, because the school day was almost over. What could he do?

<h1 style="text-align:center">5</h1>

After school, the three boys gathered together at the front of the school.

Chris and Eric were razzing on how much trouble that they were going to get David into. David pleaded, worrying that he would get suspended. And he had already fallen back a tad due to the uncontrolled memories of his father (John) running through his mind like a rapidly spinning wheel.

The three came to an understanding. One that David was not happy about. Chris and Eric had stated that if David got a candy bar, so should they.

About two blocks from the school there was a convenience store that the three boys were walking to. David was nervous. He would miss the bus ride home, but maybe his mother would pick him up after he would ultimately lie about his mischievous actions. He had much more to worry about once entering the store that the three speedily walked to without saying much. Practically nothing, actually.

Chris and Eric waited outside because a deal had been made.

"You go in and get me a chocolate bar with peanuts and Eric wants some taffy. We'll be here waiting." The trouble making Chris threatened that if David refused, they would tell.

David swallowed hard as his hands began to tremble when he opened the glass door to the store. He began to look around at all the candy in isle three. He was not tempted, rather practically forced.

When the middle-aged man behind the counter turned his back to refill the lottery scratchers, David seized his opportunity. He snagged the two bars of sugar filled treats with sweaty palms. The ones that Chris and Eric had requested.

After stuffing the bars in his back, right pocket David rushed out the door with the store worker still having his back turned. When he had gotten outside, the three boys walked along the side of the building and that's when the two instigators praised and practically idolized David for his bravery.

"Not bad." Eric stated. "You're cool." Words spoken from a boy who got what he wanted.

David felt panic in his chest, but exhilaration in his heart as it beat rapidly. Now he was accepted. Now he was looked at differently. But something was brewing inside of him.

His mother arrived at the school to find her son sweating profusely after he made his way back.

"Are you okay? You look horrible. Is something wrong?" asked Julie. "Yes, I'm fine. Sorry I got you nervous mom. And no nothing's wrong." David responded to his distressed mother.

Amongst the lies, there was one which was especially bothersome. Something was wrong because he felt something that he had never felt before... The rush of adrenaline and the need to feel this same way again.

The future held many possibilities and David had two boys that put a fire in his belly. A fire that burned deep inside. And now David had a want, no, a need to shoplift again. He was very confused, but confusion would not stop what he had plans for.

For the first time, David felt the feeling of addiction. The very strong and intense emotions of a child trying to fit in by disobeying. And unfortunately, more trouble was to come, and this trouble would intensify with time and a newfound energy.

6

As the weeks went by, David spent more time and less money on his new hobby, shoplifting. He also spent some time with the two boys that lit the fire inside of him that was there all along just waiting to be woken.

Trips to the grocery store with his mother, walks to the convenient store and basically any shop that lacked in the security department, he took advantage of. It did not matter what the item was. Small or large, he had to have it. And, in his mind, he figured, why pay when I can get it for free?

The temptations never left his brain.

One day, a Wednesday in February, he had been craving a nice, cold pop. The caffeinated kind that his mother did not allow him. But he never got a chance to break the rules this day, yet.

While inside the school, counting the minutes until he would become free and independent. This once shy boy had become invigorated and grew a new sense of self-confidence. Before he had the chance to break free from the building, he received a call from his mother.

Julie had become ill and needed David to take the bus home so he could take care of Tucker while she was resting. The innocence that he had once had, came back to him, knowing he had to help his mom with an important task. He knew his mother was relying on him, so he gave himself a kick in the ass and took on the task his mother had asked of him.

Once home after the bus ride, David had seen the condition his mother was in. She was pale and weak with a very high fever. He was worried. She was even too weak to talk at this point.

So, out of panic, he gave his father a call for help. But his dad did not answer the phone, John did. There was a big difference even though it was the same person. Dad cared about Julie and David. John did not.

After asking for advice and help, he found John to be useless, so David ended the phone call, which would be the absolute last one that he would have with him. Not knowing what to do next, he speedily dialed three numbers... 911.

The ambulance had taken Julie to the hospital, while David had to stay home and look after his clingy golden retriever. Then, it hit him. He blamed himself for not thinking of calling his grandparents (Julie's parents).

Hours had passed, slowly as worries filled his mind like an overinflated balloon ready to pop. Fearing the worst, David vowed to never shoplift again as long as his precious mother came home safe. Seconds after making the vow, he received a phone call. It was his grandpa. He began to explain that the fever had broken, and Julie was doing much better, and he would be picking David up and would be bringing him to see Julie.

"Oh my god! It worked!" David exclaimed after ending the call with his grandfather. David made a promise that came from pure hope and anxiety. He would never shoplift again. Well, technically he would do as he promised, but sneaking and stealing was still in the young boy's future.

David had become a rule bender rather than a rule breaker. Was there a difference? Something was waiting for him at the hospital. Something that would change the course of his life forever. And he did not even know.

As time passed, David had gotten his ride from his grandpa, and he would be arriving at the local hospital where his mother and his fate were waiting for him.

7

"I gotta stop. I need to stop. I promised. But what will Chris and Eric do, or think, or say. I'll have no friends, again. It's mom. I have to do it for her. Plus, I don't want to get arrested. I'll be fine. I made a promise, and I will keep it. My mom better be okay."

Many back and forth thoughts, which fought against each other inside of him.

David once again had the hamster wheel effect going on in his mind. Trying to keep his words true. Abe (David's grandfather) had already picked him up and they were at the parking ramp at the hospital. Dark and dingy. Very creepy. Like something bad would happen there, but the "something" that would happen in the negative sense, would come from inside the hospital on floor number five.

Now it was time to visit his mother, who happened to be his whole world. Especially after the divorce. He did not want to let her down, even though she knew nothing in regard to shoplifting or the vow. He figured With her around, healthy and happy, nothing bad could happen. Could it?

8

David had made it to his mother's bedside while Abe was getting some goodies from the cafeteria of the hospital. David, the poor thing, had not eaten all day. He didn't have much of an appetite, but his grandfather insisted.

The mother and son were holding hands (as the two were very close) and David began to tear up at the sight of his mom in a hospital bed, even though she had improved a substantial amount.

"Sweetie don't cry. Everything is okay. I'm okay. How's Tucker doing, that little pest?" Julie asked jokingly, trying to get her one and only son to break free from fearful emotionality. It worked.

The duo were having just small talk while Abe was surprisingly taking quite a long time, at least thirty five minutes. As time and talk went by, David had an urge to urinate, but he hated public bathrooms because of his shy bladder, let alone an ER bathroom. He didn't even go at school, just home.

His mother encouraged him to just try and push through the anxiety and go to the bathroom down the hall. The encouragement somehow worked.

David had walked down the hallway on the hard, cold, green surface of the floor and used the restroom. But on his way back he had seen someone who looked familiar. But he couldn't figure out why.

An old man lay in a hospital bed with "Frank Coolie" written on a white board in his ER room. Nobody was with him at the moment, but David soon enough was as he saw a burgundy, leather-bound book with shiny pages that drew a glare from the beaming sunlight.

David made his way silently into the man's room. He looked through the book, very intrusively. There was an inscription. It read, "To Grandpa, Love Maria."

David was tempted to take the book, but then remembered the vow and set it back down. After further contemplation, David made himself believe that it was not shoplifting, just taking. So, he grabbed the book once again and began to walk away. The old man was unconscious.

All of a sudden, just as David had left the old man's room with the book, the old man flatlined. He was dead and there was no bringing him back.

With medical personnel quickly on their way, David speedily walked down the hall to his mother's room while stuffing the book in the medium sized, brown bookbag that he had brought with him.

What David did not know was that this day was not just an ordinary one. This day would forever change his life, as the old man's (Frank Coolie) had ended.

9

Julie had to spend the night at the hospital for further evaluation, so David would be spending the night at his grandparents' large cabin like house. He did love it there, but his mother was on his mind.

The doctors explained to the whole family that Julie was suffering from hemolytic anemia. A disease that the woman was unfortunate enough to be born with. It usually hits later in a person's life, which in this case happened thirty-four years after her birth.

The big words scared the young boy and also bothered Julie's parents. There were many tests that still had to be taken, but the outlook did not seem grim.

After the long, emotionally exhausting day, David was laying on Abe's futon in his office of this wooden paneled paradise. It was familiar, but it was not home.

While his back pressed on the firm futon, the phone rang, which made David pop right out of sleeping position. His mother would be coming home in the afternoon on the following day. Discharged with instructions on how to deal with this hidden disease.

"Wow. I didn't think it would work, but it did. My vow worked!" David continued on. "I guess the book really didn't matter. I knew it would. I didn't take anything of value. He was dead anyway." David spoke with an abrupt lack of emotion and no consideration. But he was wrong. He did steal something of value, he just did not know it yet.

"Why not keep taking stuff? Mom's okay." The ignorant child had not learned his lesson. As he spoke to himself, which was a little odd that he had to convince himself aloud, he took a small handful of loose change from upon his grandpa's desk. "Nothing's gonna happen." Hopefully the boy did not jinx himself.

10

Woken by the soft voice of his mother, David jumped up quickly, not expecting to see his mother until later in the afternoon, but it was only ten in the morning.

"Surprise sweetie. Did you miss me?" Of coarse David did and Julie knew it. He did not speak a word at first. He just gave his mother a tight, gripping hug, that spoke miles more than words.

With his narrow chin on his mom's shoulder David saw the book that he had so rudely taken from the old man and realized that his mom would ask questions on how it had come into his possession.

David urged his mother into the kitchen where he promised to make her her favorite breakfast. The only one that David could cook by himself, scrambled eggs and Italian toast. She lit right up as she realized the sincerity of her son. But that sincerity was false. Just a way to rid his mother from the room so he could hide the book that was peeking out of his bag.

He loved his mother very much so he gave a little off coarse direction to save his own ass, but he did already have a surprise meal planned. So, you could say he was halfway sincere.

She was waiting at the kitchen table made of solid oak while David stuffed the book under the futon and then proceeded to make his mother a breakfast.

The book was hidden, but not forgotten. He would be bringing it home with him and along with the spare coins on Abe's desk, it would not be the last thing that David stole.

11

After a weekend spent solely by his mother's side, Monday had approached, and David was going back to school for another five days of hell. But his hell was going to get a lot worse.

In Mrs. Dougley's purse that was set next to her desk were two one-dollar bills. As he swiftly and unknowingly moved, it was much too obvious.

"DAVID!" his teacher yelled. "Did you just do what I thought you did?!" David answered as if he were innocent. "No." Mrs. Dougley was appalled at the action and the lie that David had just created.

After being sent to the principal's office, he was scolded hard and for a long period of time. All of this leading to a phone call to his still recuperating mother and three days in In School Detention.

The first day of suspension was to start on this exact day, as the day had commenced not long before David's attempt to steal two lousy dollars.

Sitting in a blank, pale, white cubicle, David did not feel like doing much of anything, which was ironically the point of detention.

Pissed off for being caught for the first time, David, while still seated, gave his bookbag a hefty kick and he now reads the title "The Forgotten Soul" on the cover of the book that spilled out.

Before picking it up, Eric happened to be in the cubicle next to David and gave big props for actually trying to steal money. Money, the thing that makes the world go round.

"You got guts." Eric whispered. Then, David gave a sly wink of his left eye.

David then retrieved the novel from the stained, tan carpet and set it on the desk in front of him.

Hours had passed, and they did so slowly. So very slowly.

After the boredom had gotten to his head, David opened the book and began to read the first chapter. It was good. He actually enjoyed it.

The chapter was about a woman who had a long-lost son who secretly had put money aside for him, knowing one day that she would be seeing him again. Just a Prologue, but David did not know what that word meant, so he just called it chapter one.

David read on to the actual chapters and found himself liking a book for once. Most children have a hard time finding their first favorite book, as did David. But now, so far, he had found his.

After reading for about two hours, the school day had ended and Julie was at the front of the school outside of her car, waiting to give her son a piece of her mind about his actions. Upon first greeting him, she yanked his bag out of his grasp and found it to be quite heavy. She unzipped it to find the book.

"And what is this?" Julie asked. And her son had convinced her that it was a gift from Chris.

Before looking inside of the book, the two entered Julie's SUV. While driving, she had been saying some pretty intense chores that her son would be doing. "You're going to earn those two dollars, young man. He was only half listening, though.

While getting the ass chewing of a lifetime, David slowly ripped the inscription out of the corner of the front page. "To Grandpa, Love Maria", gone. Maybe she'll actually believe the lie about a gift from Chris. Maybe.

12

Later that night, after all of the household duties were fulfilled by David, his mother sat him down to have a serious, heart-to-heart conversation. Unfortunately, David's mind was wandering before a loud snap of the fingers in his face by Julie. She was pissed. David had only seen her get like that with John.

After getting his attention, Julie was in the middle of informing David that she had plans to work overtime because she had a small amount of money she had been putting away for him. If that was able to happen, he had to be a straight arrow and not mess up her working schedule. She was planning on working a lot after getting her health corrected and addressed.

"Really? You have money saved for me?" David asked out of wonderment and felt a familiar event was happening. "Yes! Of course!" she exclaimed.

David then began to tell his mother about the book he was reading and the similarity of a mother having funds for their sons. Julie brushed it off because she had too much more to worry over. Specifically, the stealing.

"I don't care what you read!" she snapped, trying desperately to get through to him. "It's just a coincidence. Face reality David."

David knew it was just a fluke, but the upcoming days would prove to be bigger and bigger coincidences that had David asking himself if that is what they were. Flukes?... Hopefully, but doubtful in his gut. The truth will come out.

13

The next day, reading was on the agenda as David was to spend another day in detention. He had read a great amount on this particular day, about fifty pages on consistent reading. Then, he received a message to report to the front office.

"You got to be kidding me! I didn't do anything wrong!" That was true. This trip to the office was for his mom delivering a message to him in person in a plain, dull, spare office.

"Hey sweetie." She began. As the conversation went on, it was all too familiar.

John had died. At only age thirty-nine, he had suffered a stroke that took his life. The doctors could not even explain how this came to be. All of his functions were perfect. How a stroke came to be was unknown. But, David believed more flukes were becoming too real to handle.

David broke down and started crying. He sobbed hard and began to rant.

"I should have known. I should have warned someone. It's all too real!" "How do you mean too real?" Julie asked in a gentle voice. A lot less gentle than she was the night before.

Her son began to speak of what he read in his new book. A middle aged, divorced man dying of multiple strokes. David was starting to get freaked out at the two consecutive incidences that were all too familiar.

Whether it was dad or John, he was deceased. And so far, things were becoming very eerie and making David question if reality and the book differed, or if they were connected.

The shoplifting had slowed down considerably as David had invested himself in reading his first favorite book. But which was worse. That was currently unknown.

14

In the next few days, creepy things began happening. In the book and in real life. But were they two of the same.

The book took twists and turns as the main character began noticing things misplaced or going missing, sounding in the night. Ghastly sounds. It took a ghostly turn.

There was no problem with reading the novel, but when the actions in the book rang true to what was happening in his real life, David became afraid.

One night after setting the book on the nightstand, David fell asleep and dreamed the worst of nightmares. Being the worst because of the man he saw. The old man in his dream was the same old man who had his book stolen by David. The dead man.

Frank Coolie. He remembered the name on the whiteboard.

The dream was of Frank Coolie kissing his granddaughter goodbye as she slipped into the deep slumber of death.

"I stole his book. I'm fucked." David got one thing right. A haunting had begun, and it was due to his sneaky hobby. The hobby that brought nothing but trouble.

David, freaking out, throws the book in the garbage. But that only made the noises louder, and the chills colder. It was getting worse rather than the opposite.

The night after throwing out the book, David had another nightmare of Frank Coolie. "FINISH!" Frank demanded in the dream. David just got an idea after waking in the middle of the night drenched in sweat.

"Maybe if I finish the book, the haunting will stop." David thought. He immediately went to the kitchen garbage and retrieved the book and obsessively tried to finish it as fast as his brain allowed him to. But things kept getting worse.

David had the name, Frank Coolie stamped on his brain.

After researching on the internet, he found a phone number of Frank Coolie's last known address. It was time to make a phone call.

15

A woman answered the phone. Martha Coolie was her name. The widow of Frank Coolie. After questions from David, Martha told him what he already knew.

Months before, David had dreamed of a cancer victim gifting a book to her grandfather just before passing. That dream was not a dream.

It seemed as if it was meant to be, but in the worst way. This event really happened and when David stole the book from the old man (Frank Coolie), he might as well have pulled the plug. David killed him and now Frank wanted to settle the score.

After more research, David finds where Frank is buried. Only four miles away. A long walk for a young boy. He did not care, he slipped out of the house in the mid hours of the night and walked to Frank Coolie's headstone.

There it was. The name Frank Coolie carved just above a collection of flowers. The little bastard had the nerve to actually steal some of the flowers for his mother after pleading to Frank to leave him alone.

In the morning, the now very healthy Julie had flowers waiting for her on the table and David had a book to finish.

16

A horrible storm had come on just after finishing the book. And feeling like he may be at ease, David fell asleep. Then, he thought he was having another nightmare, but once again reality came ferociously.

The novel flew on the floor and began to glow bright, lime green. Then, the beloved book disintegrated into blood. A blood puddle on David's hardwood floor. Then, there was Frank right there in front of David. A dead man in the flesh ready to deliver a message.

David was frozen with fear. And Frank began to speak.

The scolding was given to David. A scolding of a lifetime. Explained was, once David finished the book, Frank's soul was freed after being condemned in it at the point of when it was stolen.

Now, Frank explained that he was to take David's soul and damn it to hell until once fully read again. Then Frank was gone.

David became blood on the floor and formed into the book itself. "The Forgotten Soul". That is where David is.

David shoplifted and stole. Stealing left and right. But Frank taking David's soul was the ultimate steal. "To Grandpa, Love Maria." That's where it all started and ended.

The End

Thank you to all readers for choosing my story!

Don't miss out!

Visit the website below and you can sign up to receive emails whenever Nicholas James Zornow publishes a new book. There's no charge and no obligation.

https://books2read.com/r/B-A-JBNX-DAPRC

BOOKS 2 READ

Connecting independent readers to independent writers.

Did you love *The Ultimate Steal*? Then you should read *Beneath The Secret Oak Tree*[1] by Nicholas James Zornow!

Beneath The Secret Oak Tree

By

Nicholas James Zornow

[2]

A teenage girl goes through twists and turns in her personal life as skeletons crawl from their closets and reveals much.
Read more at www.books2read.com/njz.

---

1. https://books2read.com/u/4jEAVD

2. https://books2read.com/u/4jEAVD

Also by Nicholas James Zornow

Beneath The Secret Oak Tree
Midnight Fright Fest
Personal Poetry
They'll All Fall Down
The Ultimate Steal
Me, Not Being Me
A Conversation With Myself
Silently Violent
From My Shallow Beating Heart
Three Of Me
Untitled
The Untold Stories Of...
Mr. C
The Cloud Of Christmas Day
Life With Love
Heartbeats
A Trip To The Devil's Hole
Everything Will Be Alright In The Morning
Populate
Tales from Nick
Red Rose Promise

Watch for more at www.books2read.com/njz.

About the Author

Nicholas James Zornow is an author from upstate New York. He has many stories available all over the world. His influences are authors like Edgar Allan Poe, Ambrose Bierce, Stephen King and H.G. Wells. He loves writing and aspires to be just as great as the authors he looks up to.

Read more at www.books2read.com/njz.